Barbara Reid

The Night Before Christmas

Poem by
Clement C. Moore

Albert Whitman & Company
Chicago, Illinois

The illustrations in this book were made with Plasticine
that was shaped and pressed onto illustration board. Paint and
other materials were used for special effects.
The type is set in Century Schoolbook.
Photography by Ian Crysler.

Library of Congress Cataloging-in-Publication data
is on file with the publisher.

Illustrations copyright © 2013 by Barbara Reid
First published in Canada by North Winds Press,
an imprint of Scholastic Canada Ltd.
Published in 2014 by Albert Whitman & Company
ISBN 978-0-8075-5625-2

Printed in China.
10 9 8 7 6 5 4 3 2 1 NP 18 17 16 15 14

For more information about Albert Whitman & Company,
visit our web site at www.albertwhitman.com.

For children and mice,
both naughty and nice
   —B.R.

'Twas the night before Christmas,
when all through the house
Not a creature was stirring,
not even a mouse.

The stockings were hung
by the chimney with care,
In hopes that St. Nicholas
soon would be there.

The children were nestled
all snug in their beds,

While visions of sugarplums
danced in their heads;

And Mamma in her 'kerchief, and I in my cap,
Had just settled down for a long winter's nap,

When out on the lawn there arose such a clatter,
I sprang from the bed to see what was the matter.

Away to the window I flew like a flash,

Tore open the shutters and threw up the sash.

The moon on the breast of the new-fallen snow,

Gave a lustre of midday to objects below,

When, what to my wondering eyes did appear,

But a miniature sleigh and eight tiny reindeer,

With a little old driver so lively and quick,

I knew in a moment he must be St. Nick.

More rapid than eagles his coursers they came,
And he whistled, and shouted, and called them by name:
"Now, Dasher! Now, Dancer! Now, Prancer and Vixen!
On, Comet! On, Cupid! On, Donder and Blitzen!
To the top of the porch! To the top of the wall!
Now dash away! Dash away! Dash away all!"

As leaves that before the wild hurricane fly,
When they meet with an obstacle, mount to the sky;
So up to the housetop the coursers they flew,

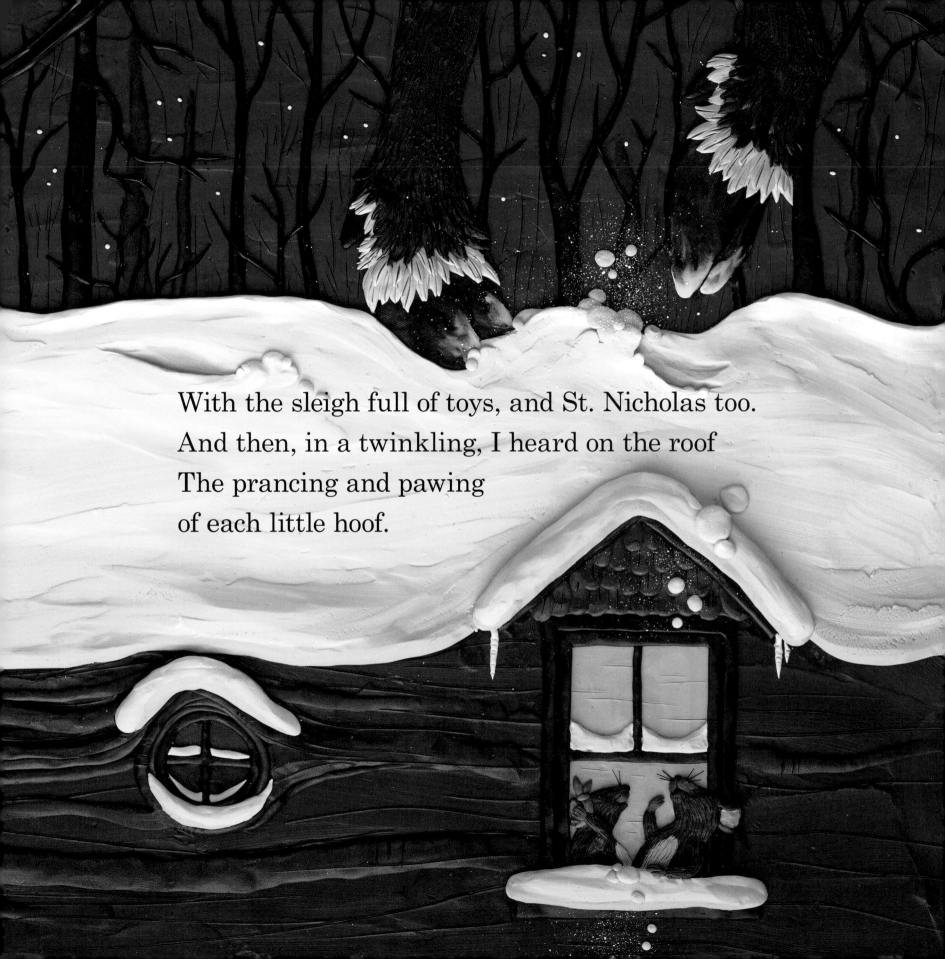

With the sleigh full of toys, and St. Nicholas too.
And then, in a twinkling, I heard on the roof
The prancing and pawing
of each little hoof.

As I drew in my head, and was turning around,
Down the chimney St. Nicholas came with a bound.
He was dressed all in fur, from his head to his foot,
And his clothes were all tarnished with ashes and soot.
A bundle of toys he had flung on his back,
And he looked like a peddler just opening his pack.

His eyes—how they twinkled! His dimples, how merry!

His cheeks were like roses, his nose like a cherry!

His droll little mouth was drawn up like a bow,

And the beard on his chin was as white as the snow.

The stump of a pipe he held tight in his teeth,

And the smoke, it encircled his head like a wreath.

He had a broad face and a little round belly,

That shook when he laughed, like a bowl full of jelly.

He was chubby and plump,
a right jolly old elf,
And I laughed when I saw him,
in spite of myself.
A wink of his eye
and a twist of his head,
Soon gave me to know
I had nothing to dread.

He spoke not a word,
but went straight to his work,

And filled all the stockings;
then turned with a jerk,

And laying his finger
aside of his nose,
And giving a nod,
up the chimney he rose.
He sprang to his sleigh,
to his team gave a whistle,
And away they all flew
like the down of a thistle.

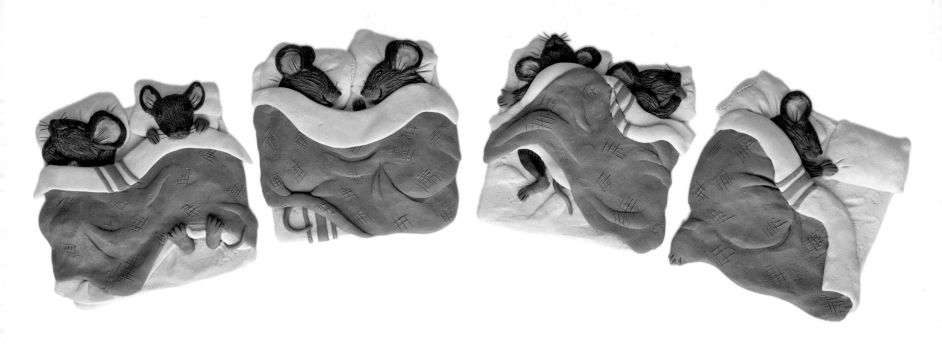

But I heard him exclaim, ere he drove out of sight,
"Merry Christmas to all, and to all a good night."